LEVEL 2 READER

The Magic School Bus Rides Again

Blowing in the Wind

Scholastic

ISBN 978-1-338-25377-1

10 9 8 7 6 5 4 3 19 20 21 22
Printed in the U.S.A. 40

First printing 2018
Book design by Jessica Meltzer

Meet Ms. Frizzle!
No other science teacher is quite like her.
She takes her class on wild field trips.
They go on her Magic School Bus.
It twirls and whirls and can go anywhere.
Where will the bus take them today?

Ms. Frizzle's class is putting on a play called *The Three Little Pigs*. Keesha is in charge of the play. Everyone works together to build the **set**.

Keesha wants everything to be perfect and look as real as possible.

"The brick house needs to stand up to the huffing and puffing wolf who tries to blow it down," she tells the class.

"But how do we learn how to build a super-strong house?" asks Ralphie.

"A field trip!" Keesha shouts.

"I knew she'd say that," jokes Ralphie.

"To the Magic School Bus!" cries Ms. Frizzle.

“Bus, do your stuff!” Ms. Frizzle calls.

The bus twirls and whirls. It lands on top of a mountain in a flash of magic.

“If we’re building a house, we need bricks,” says Keesha.

“So why are we on a mountaintop?” asks Jyoti.

"It's a surprise," says Ms. Frizzle.

Then Ms. Frizzle presses a button and POOF! The bus transforms into a brick-making machine.

“How did the bus do that?” asks Jyoti.

“It’s magic! Just go with it,” says Ms. Frizzle.

“If we use heavy bricks, nothing will be able to blow down our house,” says Keesha.

“Heavy bricks sound like a great idea,” says Carlos.

“Until you have to carry them,” groans Wanda.

Ms. Frizzle's class starts stacking bricks. They line up one brick on top of another until they make a tall tower.

"This field trip is hard work!" says Tim.

The class finishes building the house.

"Wahooo!" they shout.

"Now we need to test it," says Ms. Frizzle.

"Why do we need to do that?" Keesha asks. "This building is super strong!"

“According to my research, **engineers** don’t just hope that the buildings they make are strong. They test them to make sure,” says D.A.

So Ms. Frizzle turns on the bus’s powerful fan.

The strong wind from the fan nearly blows away the kids. It also makes the house blow down.

"Oh no! It's raining bricks!" says Wanda.

“That was amazing!” says Ms. Frizzle.

“What? It was a total disaster!” says Arnold.

“I think Ms. Frizzle means that we can learn from our mistakes,” says Jyoti.

“Let’s start over!” shouts Keesha.
“We need to stick the bricks together.”

“I have just the thing,” says Ms. Frizzle.

The bus makes a sticky material like glue.

“Goop?” the kids ask.

“It’s magic **mortar**!” she said.

The kids lay down a brick and cover it with mortar.

Then they stick another brick on top. They stack and stick the bricks until the house is finally built. The class is exhausted.

"I'm so tired my shoelaces hurt," jokes Ralphie.

The second house needs to be tested. This time, Ms. Frizzle gives the kids special glasses to see the wind and turns on the fan.

Oh no! The new house blows down, too.

“We have to try again! We need more than just heavy bricks and mortar,” says Keesha.

But the class is too tired. They want the field trip to be over.

Everyone gets on the bus to go home. The bus starts to lift off the ground.

"But you have to stay and help!" Keesha yells. She tries to hit the STOP button to make the class stay. But she hits a different button instead.

Suddenly, Keesha and Ms. Frizzle are all alone on the bus.

The button turned the bus and Keesha's friends into trees!

"Well, you did want to stop them from going home," says Ms. Frizzle.

"But I didn't want them to become trees!" cries Keesha.

"Look, a storm is coming! The wind will blow down the trees just like it blew down our house!" shouts Keesha. "We have to help our friends."

"They'll be okay," says Ms. Frizzle. "And now we can see wind in action."

The wind blows and blows, but the trees do not fall over.

"But how are trees stronger than a brick house?" asks Keesha.

"Let's find out," says Ms. Frizzle.

Keesha puts on her special glasses.

“I can see the wind sliding around the trunks,” says Keesha.

“Hey, that tickles,” laughs Arnold.

“We have roots underground. They’re holding us in place,” says D.A.

“And we are **swaying** in the wind instead of falling over,” says Arnold.

“Wow! The wind can’t blow us down!” says D.A.

After the storm, the kids turn back to normal.

They have ideas about how to make their house as strong as a tree.

"It should have a **foundation** like roots," says Tim.

"And round curves like a tree trunk," says D.A.

"Let's make the mortar **flexible** so the house sways in the wind," says Jyoti.

The Magic School Bus takes
the kids back to school and digs
a hole for the house's foundation.

Then the kids get to work.
Soon the house is built!

Now it's showtime! Ralphie is dressed like the wolf. He pretends to blow down the house just as Ms. Frizzle turns on the bus's fan. Will the house blow down?

The wind slides around the round sides.
The foundation acts like roots.
The new mortar makes the house sway.
The house does not blow down!

Later, the kids read a **review** of their play.

It says, "Don't see the play. It's too scary and too windy!"

"Who's going to come see the play now?" asks Arnold.

"Everyone!" shouts Keesha. "The review made it sound so exciting that the play is sold out! We did it together!"

"Wahooo!" shouts the class.

Professor Frizzle's Glossary

Hi, I'm Ms. Frizzle's sister, Professor Frizzle. I used to teach at Walkerville Elementary. Now I do scientific research with my sidekick, Goldie. I'm always on an adventure learning new things, so here are some words for you to learn, too! Wahooo!

engineer: A person who designs and builds things

flexible: Capable of bending

foundation: A stone or concrete structure that supports a building from underneath

mortar: A thick paste used to hold brick or stone together

review: A report that gives an opinion about a play, book, or movie

set: The furniture, scenery, and backdrop of a play

swaying: Moving slowly back and forth